The
Radio Station
Mystery

Elaine Pageler

High Noon Books
Novato, California

Cover Design and Interior Illustrations: Tina Cash

International Standard Book Number: 0-87879-987-7

9 8 7 6 5 4 3 2 1 0
4 3 2 1 0 9 8 7 6 5

Contents

CHAPTER 1

The File Cabinet

Brad started his car and headed for work. He turned on the radio.

"I am Big Al. This is Station WNAZ. Stay tuned for our Fun Night drawing. But let's have some music first," a man's voice said.

The music was good. It put Brad in a happy mood. He hummed along and drove down the street. Up ahead was the News. Brad pulled into the parking lot. He got out and went inside.

Meg stood beside her desk. It was a mess.

She had pulled things out of the drawers. It was all on top of the desk.

She saw him. "Where have you been? I need your help," she said.

"What are you doing?" Brad asked.

Meg led him to the back room. She pointed to an old file cabinet. "Look what I got. The boss gave it to me," she said.

"Where did that come from?" Brad asked.

"The News bought some old file cabinets from Station WNAZ. They're getting new ones. Help me move it to my desk," Meg said.

They moved the cabinet. Brad did most of the work. He wasn't in a good mood now.

Brad was tired. He sat down to rest.

Meg put her things inside. But she still didn't look happy.

"Now what's wrong?" Brad asked.

"It's broken. The bottom drawer won't close," Meg said.

Brad looked at it. The drawer stuck out a bit. No one else would mind. But Meg did. She was like that.

"Let me look at it," he said.

Brad pulled out the drawer. He reached in with his hand. His fingers felt something. It was crumpled paper. He pulled it out.

"Here's why it didn't close. Some paper was in there," he said.

Brad handed Meg the paper. There were

*"Here's why it didn't close.
Some paper was in there," Brad said.*

two pieces. Then he put the drawer back in.

Meg looked at them. "This must belong to Station WNAZ. One is a picture of a man. I think it's Big Al. The other is a list of four names. It tells where they live, too," Meg said.

Brad looked at the list. "That's a bad typewriter. All the M's are dark. Guess what? The last name is my aunt and uncle," he said.

"Brad! Meg!" called a voice. It was their boss. He walked over to them.

"There has been a robbery. Bob was to cover it. But he's been sick. I can't wait any longer. I'm giving it to you. Write a story and get some pictures. Here's the name," he said.

The boss dropped the sheet of paper on

Meg's desk. Then he walked off.

Meg read it. Then she looked at the other paper on her desk.

"That's what I thought. The Dodd's name is on the file cabinet list, too," she said. "Their name is just above your aunt and uncle's name. Maybe your aunt and uncle will be robbed next."

Brad knew she was joking. He made a face at her. "Very funny," he said.

CHAPTER 2

Station WNAZ

Brad picked up his camera. He and Meg went out to the car. They were going to see the Dodds. Brad started the car and turned on the radio.

"This is Big Al from Station WNAZ. Stay tuned. Our Fun Night drawing is coming up. Here's more music," the man said.

"There's Station WNAZ up ahead. Let's stop and drop off their papers," Meg said.

Brad shook his head. "You just want to talk

to Big Al. But there's no time. We have a story to do."

"Don't you want to know about the Dodds? Their names were on that list," Meg said.

Brad had been thinking about that. Talking to WNAZ might be a good idea.

He pulled into the parking lot. They got out and walked inside.

A young woman sat at the desk. A man leaned across it. He was talking to her.

Meg stepped forward. "Liz, is that you?" she asked.

The young woman looked up. A smile broke out on her face. "Why, it's Meg Green. I haven't seen you since school. I've read your stories in the News," she said.

Meg smiled. "This is Brad. He works with me," she said.

Liz shook hands with Brad. She turned to the man near her desk. "This is Ed. He's my boyfriend," she said.

"It's nice to meet you," Ed said.

Meg told Liz about the file cabinet. She pulled out the picture. "Brad found this behind the drawer," she said.

Liz looked at the picture. So did Ed.

"That's Big Al. It must have been his file cabinet. I'll give it to him," Liz said.

"I like meeting Liz's friends. But it's time to get back to work. What are you two doing tonight? Can we all meet at the Blue Pine for dinner?" Ed asked.

"That sounds good. Doesn't it, Brad?" Meg asked.

"Sure," Brad said. What else could he say?

"Good, we'll meet you at 7 o'clock," Ed said. He went out the door.

The station manager came out of his room. He picked up the box on the table. "Come on, Liz. It's time for the drawing," he said.

Liz jumped up. "It's for the WNAZ Fun Night. Come and watch. Maybe you'll win," she said. Brad and Meg went along. They all walked down the hall.

On the way, Meg asked, "By the way, Liz,

who won Fun Night last week?"

"I think their name was Dodd," Liz said.

A man was inside a glass room. He talked into a mike. "This is Big Al from Station WNAZ. It's time for our Fun Night drawing," he said.

The manager opened the door. He gave Big Al the box. Big Al shook it near the mike. Then he pulled out a slip of paper. "The winners are Mr. and Mrs. Cook," he said.

A cold chill ran up Brad's back. That was his aunt and uncle's name.

CHAPTER 3

The Robbery

Brad and Meg left WNAZ. They headed for the Dodds. The drawing was still on their mind.

"We find a list from Station WNAZ. It has four names on it. Two of them won the Fun Night drawing. Did the others win it, too?" Brad asked.

"Stop! There's a phone. I'll find out," Meg told him.

Brad saw the phone. He slammed on the brakes. His tires squealed. He pulled over.

Meg jumped out and rushed to the phone. She came back soon. A frown was on her face.

"What did you find out?" Brad asked.

"We guessed it. All of them won the WNAZ drawing. There's something else, too. Each was robbed," Meg told him.

Brad was shocked. "Are you sure?" he asked.

"Yes. The first family was robbed two weeks ago. The next was robbed last week. The Dodds were robbed this week," Meg said.

"Some people may be robbed next week, too. They will be my aunt and uncle," Brad said.

Meg nodded. "That could be. The winners go to the Fun Night. Their house is empty. That makes it safe for the robbers," Meg said.

Brad drove to the Dodd's house. He and Meg got out. They walked up to the house.

Mr. Dodd opened the door. He looked upset.

Brad showed him his press card. "We're from the News. Could we talk to you? It's about the robbery," he said.

The man led them inside. His wife sat in a chair. Her eyes were red.

"The robbers took all my jewelry. Our silver is gone, too," she said.

"How did they get in?" Brad asked.

"The police found a window open. They think we forgot to lock it," Mr. Dodd told them.

"That's wrong. It's always locked. We don't open it," Mrs. Dodd said.

"You had been to the WNAZ Fun Night. Did you have a good time?" Meg asked.

"Yes, it was great. The WNAZ people came out. They gave us tickets. They were to Rancho Burr. I should have worn my new jewelry. But Big Al said not to dress up," Mrs. Dodd said.

"When did they give you the tickets?" Brad asked.

"It was the same day," Mrs. Dodd said.

"We went out to Rancho Burr. Some of the WNAZ people were there. We had dinner with them. Then there was a play and dancing. We got home late," Mr. Dodd said.

Brad gave Meg a look. Then he turned back to Mrs. Dodd. "Was Big Al there?" he asked.

"He and his girlfriend came late. The show had started," Mrs. Dodd said.

Brad took a picture. Then he and Meg thanked the Dodds and left.

They drove to the police station. Sergeant Ward seemed glad to see them.

"What can I do for you?" he asked.

Meg showed him the list from the file cabinet. "These people were robbed. Weren't they?"

Sergeant Ward looked at the list. "Three of them were. But I don't know anything about the Cooks," he said.

"We think they will be robbed, too," Brad said. He told Sergeant Ward about the list and the Fun Night drawing.

Sergeant Ward looked at the list again. "All of them told me they were gone for the night. But they didn't tell me why. We had other clues," he said.

"What other clues?" Brad asked.

"There's something else about those people. All of them had bought something from Robb's Jewelry Store. It cost a lot. The robbers took it," Sergeant Ward told them.

Brad's heart started to beat fast. His uncle had just bought his aunt a ring. It was from Robb's Store, too.

CHAPTER 4

The Jewelry Store

Brad and Meg drove up the street. They headed back to the News. There was work to do. The boss wanted their story.

Station WNAZ was on the next block. Brad turned on the radio. Big Al might be talking. But he wasn't. There was only music.

"Big Al must be on a break," he said.

Meg pointed at the sidewalk. "There's Big Al now. He's walking down the street. Where's he going?" she asked.

This block had lots of stores. Brad saw a parking place and pulled in.

"Let's follow him. He won't see us. We're on the other side of the street," Brad said.

They got out and started up the street. Big Al walked on. Then he turned and went into a store.

Brad looked at the sign. It said, "Robb's Jewelry Store."

"That's where those people on the list went. They got their jewelry from Robb's," he said.

They crossed the street and looked in. It was a small store. Only two other people were inside. The jeweler sat at a desk. He worked on a watch. The salesgirl showed Big Al rings.

Big Al held the ring in his hand. He said something in her ear. Both of them laughed.

"Let's go inside," Meg said. She walked through the door. Brad followed. There was nothing else he could do.

The jeweler got up. "What can I show you?" he asked.

"Watches," Brad said.

"Rings," Meg said.

The jeweler laughed. He patted Brad on the arm. "Women are like that. They all want rings," he said.

Brad's face got red. He turned to glare at Meg. But she was gone.

Meg had walked over to the rings. Now she

stood beside Big Al.

"Why it's Big Al from WNAZ. Did you get your picture back?" she asked.

Big Al turned to look at her. He didn't smile. "What picture?" he asked.

"I brought it over. It was in your old file cabinet," she told him.

Big Al gave the salesgirl a funny look. Then he walked to the door. "It wasn't mine. I don't have a file cabinet," he said.

Brad watched him leave. Big Al rushed down the street.

"Show these people some rings," the jeweler told the salesgirl.

The salesgirl pulled out some rings. But her

Big Al turned to look at her.

eyes looked out the window. She watched Big Al walk down the street.

Meg put on a ring. "I like this one," she said.

Brad looked at the price tag. "This ring is $2,000. That's a lot. What if someone steals it?" he asked.

The salesgirl handed him a card. "This man will insure it. That way you'll be safe," she said.

Brad put the card in his pocket. "That costs money, too. Let's go, Meg," he said.

Meg followed him outside. "I bet that's it. Big Al and the salesgirl are the robbers," she said.

"I think so, too," Brad said.

He looked back in the window. The salesgirl had the phone in her hand.

They went back to the News. Brad's phone was ringing. It was his aunt.

"Guess what? Your uncle and I won the WNAZ drawing. We're going to the Fun Night," she said.

"That's great," Brad said.

He tried to sound happy. But there was a frown on his face. Somehow he had to stop the robbers.

CHAPTER 5

Help from Liz

Brad and Meg worked as fast as they could. At last Meg's story was done. So was Brad's photo. Their story would be in the News the next day.

They just had time to get to the Blue Pine. Brad drove fast. They got there at 7 o'clock.

Liz waited at a table. She waved at them. They walked over.

"Ed had to work late. He'll be here soon," she said.

"We had to work late, too," Meg said.

"What were you doing?" Liz asked

"We had to do a story. It's for the News," Brad told her.

Meg started talking about their school days. Liz joined in. Brad laughed at their stories. Time went fast.

Ed rushed across the room. "Sorry I'm late. A man wanted his car insured. I had to meet him after work," he said.

Liz put her hand on his arm. "Ed works odd hours," she said.

"Yes, they are. But it could be worse. Once I worked for a window company. I had long hours and little pay," he said.

The waiter came. He took their order.

Meg told Liz and Ed about the News. "The boss calls us the Riddle Street team," she said.

Liz nodded. "I've read your stories. You two are good. What are you writing next?" she asked.

"I don't know. Maybe we'll do a story on WNAZ. Tell us about the Fun Night drawing," Meg said.

Liz smiled. "The Fun Night is a great idea. Big Al thought of it. Four people get a prize this month. We choose one each week. It's for their whole family. WNAZ takes them to Rancho Burr. They get dinner and a show. There's dancing, too," she said.

"How do you pick the people?" Brad asked.

Liz looked at him. "You saw that today. Everyone's name is in a box. Big Al draws one. He reads it on the air," she told them.

"So no one knows the winners until then?" Meg asked.

"That's right. It's a surprise for all of us," Liz told her.

"Is it always Big Al? Or does someone else draw the names, too?" Brad asked.

"It's Big Al's idea. He draws the names," Liz told them.

Brad glanced at Meg. Then he looked back at Liz. "What happens then?" he asked.

"I phone the winner. We set a time that's good for them," Liz said.

"Do you go to the Fun Night?" Meg asked.

Ed laughed. "They never ask Liz. I wish they would. We like to dance," he said.

"Fun Night costs a lot. So I don't mind," Liz told them.

Meg and Liz started talking about school days again. Brad looked across the room. He saw Big Al come in. The salesgirl was with him.

His name was Big Al. But he was as thin as Brad and Ed. Yes, this man might be a robber. He could climb through windows.

Ed saw Big Al, too. "Liz thinks he's great. But I don't like that guy," he said.

Dinner came. It was good. They talked and

laughed. At last Brad and Meg had to go.

"Thanks for a good time," Brad said.

"We'll do this again," Ed told them.

Brad and Meg went out to their car. They drove down Riddle Street.

"That was fun. Liz was a big help, too. She told us a lot about Station WNAZ," Meg said.

"Yes, she did. I'm putting cameras in my aunt and uncle's house," Brad said.

"What for?" Meg asked.

"WNAZ comes with the tickets. Someone opens a window. Then he comes back to rob the house. I want to know who," Brad said.

"I bet it's Big Al," Meg told him.

Brad nodded. "It could be," he said.

CHAPTER 6

The Open Window

Brad and Meg sat in the car. They talked about the robbers.

"Here's what I think. People bought jewelry from Robb's. The salesgirl told Big Al. They made a list of houses to rob," Brad said.

"Big Al got an idea. His station would have a drawing. He would use that list," Meg added.

"That's right. WNAZ brought tickets to the house. That's when Big Al unlocked a window," Brad said.

"Then the people would go to the Fun Night. No one was home. The robbers could come in. What a clever plan," Meg went on.

Brad nodded. "My aunt and uncle are next. Their Fun Night is in five days," he said.

The next day Brad phoned his aunt. She was happy. The Fun Night was all she talked about. Brad didn't want to spoil that. So he didn't tell about the robbers.

"My heater is out. It will take a week to fix it. May I stay with you?" he asked.

"Yes, come to the Fun Night with us. I'll phone WNAZ," his aunt said.

"No, I have work to do. Don't tell anyone I'm staying there," Brad told her.

Brad moved in. He waited until his aunt and uncle went to bed. Then he crept down the stairs. A video camera was in his hands.

The living room was big. The open staircase was in the back. There was a railing above. That wasn't a good place for the video. His aunt would see it.

Then Brad saw the bookcase. He hid the camera there. It would cover the whole room.

Meg met him the next day. They went to see Sergeant Ward. They told him about the camera.

"My aunt and uncle leave at 7 o'clock. The robbers will come after that. I will be in the house. The lights will be off," Brad said.

"I'll bring some men. We'll be hiding close by. Here's my two-way radio. We can talk to you," Sergeant Ward said.

"I'll be in the house, too," Meg said.

"No, stay with Sergeant Ward," Brad said.

The Fun Night came. Brad got home from work. His aunt and uncle rushed to their car. They left for Rancho Burr.

Brad took the film from the video camera. He put it in the VCR.

The pictures started. Big Al, the manager, and Liz came in. Big Al gave tickets to his aunt. Liz took out her camera. Big Al went to the window. He pulled down the shade. Liz's camera flashed. Then Big Al put up the shade.

Brad checked the window. It was unlocked.

"Is everything all right?" Meg called. Her voice came from the two-way radio.

Brad turned off the VCR.

He spoke into the radio. "I looked at the film. Big Al left the living room window open. The robbers should be here soon" he told her.

The room was dark. Brad could only see shadows. Wait! Was that a sound? Brad walked to the stairs. That's where the sound came from. Nothing was there.

"Calm down," he told himself.

Another sound came from above. Brad looked up. Something dark was falling! A net dropped over him. He couldn't get loose.

There were more sounds. Two people raced downstairs. It was too dark to see their faces.

Brad tugged at the net. He couldn't get out. Then he thought of the two-way radio.

"Help! We're being robbed!" he called

The two people rushed back upstairs. Their arms were full.

Sergeant Ward burst in a minute later.

"They're upstairs," Brad told him

Sergeant Ward ran up the stairs. He went into a room. Then he came back out.

"The side window is open. There's a ladder across to the next roof. That's why we didn't see them. The robbers came over that roof," he said.

CHAPTER 7

The Mistake

"Why didn't Big Al come in the front window?" Meg asked.

"It doesn't make sense," Brad said.

"Phone Rancho Burr. Ask your aunt and uncle to come home. I want the WNAZ people, too," Sergeant Ward told Brad.

He turned to Meg. "Many people work for WNAZ. Do you know all of them?" he asked.

"I'll phone my friend. Liz will make a list for us," Meg told him.

Sergeant Ward went upstairs. He and his men wanted to check the roof.

Brad and Meg made their phone calls. Then Brad turned on the VCR. They sat down to watch. The screen showed an empty room. None of the WNAZ people were there.

"Oh, I need to rewind the film," Brad said.

"Wait! Who is that?" Meg asked.

Brad looked at the screen. He saw his uncle and a man in a blue jacket come into the living room.

"I can't see his face," Meg said.

They kept looking at the screen. The man went around the room. He stopped at each window. Then he went upstairs. Brad heard cars outside. He turned off the VCR. His aunt and uncle and the WNAZ people rushed in.

Tears streamed down his aunt's face. "Did the robbers come in the living room window? I left it unlocked," she said.

Brad frowned. His aunt had left the window unlocked. It wasn't Big Al at all.

"What's this about? Why are we here?" Big Al asked. His arm was around the salesgirl. The manager and his family stood close by. They didn't look happy.

"Sergeant Ward wants to talk to you. He'll be down soon," Brad told them.

His aunt and uncle had gone into their room. Now they came out. She was crying.

"They took my new ring," she said.

His uncle put his arm around her. "Don't worry. I insured the ring," he said.

Brad took his uncle to one side. "Who was the man in the blue jacket on the video? He came after the WNAZ people," Brad said.

"That man was from a window company. He checked the house for winter," his uncle said.

"Did you call him?" Brad asked.

"No, he just knocked on the door," his uncle said. "Your aunt is upset. I'm going to take her back to our room."

Brad looked at Meg. She stared back at him. Both of them were thinking the same thing. The man had gone upstairs. He must have opened a window there.

A thought struck Brad. "There's an insured man and a man from a window company. Does that make you think of someone?" he asked Meg.

Meg nodded. "We made a mistake," she said.

Brad and Meg went up and talked to Sergeant Ward. Then they came back down.

The doorbell rang. Liz and Ed came in. "Here's your list," Liz said. Meg looked at the list. She smiled and gave it to Brad.

He smiled, too. "That's it," he said.

Sergeant Ward came down the stairs. "Brad and Meg have something to tell you," he said.

Meg told everyone about the list. Brad told them about the Fun Night and the robbing.

"The robbers are in this room," he said.

Everyone gasped.

"It isn't me," Big Al said.

Brad nodded. "We know that now. Someone else knew about the jewelry sales. It was the person who insured them. That person used to work for a window company. He still has his blue jacket on. It's you. Isn't it, Ed?" Brad asked.

"You're crazy!" Ed told him.

Brad went on. "The file cabinet belonged to Liz. That's how the list got there," he said.

"She fixed the drawing. All the slips of

Brad held up the two slips of paper.

paper had the same name," Meg said.

"You can't prove any of this," Liz said.

Brad held up two slips of paper. "This is the list from the file cabinet. See the dark M's. Now here's the list you typed tonight. It has dark M's, too," he said.

Liz turned on Ed. "We shouldn't have tried a robbery this week. They were on to the plan. I told you not to use that window trick. But you had to try to outsmart them."

"It's hard to outsmart Brad and Meg," Sergeant Ward said.

Brad looked at Meg. Both of them smiled. The Riddle Street team had done it again.